The Writers' Block

Michael Wheatley

The Writers' Block

Michael Wheatley
Edited by Black Pear Press

First published in May 2019 by Black Pear Press
www.blackpear.net

ISBN 978-1-910322-95-6

Cover Design by Lucas Wickens

Black Pear Press

For the Block

Contents

The Straw Man

The canopy blocks all brightness, and the vines are overgrown and still growing. The forest floor is uneven, littered with detritus, as branches break off in the wind. The woods are, and always have been, a desolate place, spiralling out in a ceaseless stream. But within, there sits a solitary village: a community enclosed by the trees.

Its folk till and toil the land, the fields ploughed into parallel rows. There are shops, a square and a couple of schools; the cobble streets always active, alive. In the communal gardens, flowers flourish in bloom, with stone statues scattered among them. But day in and day out, the folk only look up. A tower block shatters the sky.

Twenty-three storeys—same size, same shape—watch over the village below. The same whitewashed walls, the same solitary windows: each floor dissolves into another. From the highest point, smoke yawns ever higher: a reminder of life, of purpose. As the charcoal smoke seeps from the summit, the artist works towards greatness.

For the past twenty-three years, when the fields are fallow and the crops have been collected, the village takes time to reset. A fortnight is spared from the pressures of production, as the folk come alive with culture. Stands are built and stages set, to share stories, shows and spectacles. Decorations are crocheted from cottages to cabins, their bright colours drawn from the gardens. For fourteen days, tales are told and works admired, as the folk ready for the year ahead.

Then, on the final day, before the land calls for labour and the folk revert to routine, the village consumes the Great Work. Built, applauded, burned. The sky succumbs to a scarlet smoke, and the folk breathe it in; fill their lungs, their bodies, their blood with the ashes of art; store enough so that they shall sustain. The first year it had been a portrait, the twelfth a tapestry. On the eve of the twenty-third, the village awaits an effigy.

At the apex of the block, half-exhausted bales built up around him, the Straw Man hones his creations. With worn and flayed fingers, he withdraws strands of straw, folds them over into themselves, then wraps a noose around their neck. Teeth and nails sharpened to tools, the edges are cut, the feet bound and the waist cinched. The process repeats before one bisects its double and the effigy is complete. A man of straw, limbs outstretched, willing to be offered to the flame.

In the corner of the shop the furnace waits, whispering wants with crackles and cracks. With each completed piece, the Straw Man casts his work into the crucible and awaits the scarlet smoke. But the fire only coughs and splutters, exudes only pitch, and he soon starts anew.

He had come to the village the previous winter, at the end of the reset, alongside others who had flocked from afar. That year, a play had been produced, bound in leather. Over the course of twenty-one short dramas, enacted by the folk in various guises, it had chronicled an ancestry of all those artists who had come before: never seen, never heard, except through their works.

Enraptured, the village had been revived, rallied together in return to the fields. Envisioning himself among that lineage, the Straw Man had stayed: volunteered his own Great Work.

But he writhes as that work eludes him, each effigy judged wanting in heart, craft, intent. Withdraw, fold, wrap; cut, bind, cinch; pierce and burn. The furnace still roars damnation. The effigies splinter, dismantle, divide into two; individual strands of straw, then nothing. Withdraw, fold, wrap; cut, bind, cinch; pierce and burn.

The Straw Man's passion fades. He forgets what it is to create and why he thought himself creator. He stares at the bales around him, his components; looks down at his hands, his tools; concedes. The Great Work is beyond his reach. He abandons the workshop for the lower floors.

Descending the stone steps, descending into a silence disallowed by the demands of the flame, the Straw Man visits the workshops of his forebears. On the nineteenth floor, that of the novelist, he sees papers and inkwells, blank books stacked side by side; all are unused and defaulting to dust.

Further down, on the thirteenth floor, where the walls become weak and the block becomes brittle, the architect once worked. Pencils, measuring devices, and long reams of parchment once housed plans for their own Great Work. But they, too, are deserted.

The potter, the poet, the weaver; each floor a memento of their artist; a reminder of perseverance, persistence and success. In the corner of each, built one above the other, furnaces are long since slumbered.

As the Straw Man returns to his workshop, ascending the floors, he takes from each a component of their craft. A shaving of lead. A scrap of parchment. A lump of clay. In his hands, he holds the formula for his own Great Work.

He withdraws straw and dips it in the landscapist's paint; he folds it over into itself, nestling the potter's clay within; he wraps a noose around its neck using the weaver's yarn. The edges are cut with the woodcarver's knife; the feet are bound with the poet's pages; and the waist is cinched with the seamstress's tape. Satisfied at last, the Straw Man entwines the two, and the effigy is complete.

He brings it before himself and sees perfection. The clay, the paper, the lead, the straw: materials and mentors melding through him to create a new art. How the straw sits without a single loose strand, its size not too large or too small. Images of imperfections flit before him as he remembers his previous works, unfinished and unrefined. The Straw Man resists offering it to the fire, his hand charring in the furnace as he falters. But the sacrifice must be made.

As the effigy hits the flame, the furnace screams. The clay cracks, the pages shrivel; every gathered essence is destroyed in the fire, leaving only burning straw. Then the smoke starts to spread, blacker than before, enveloping the workshop and streaming out of the window. It creeps up the block and suffocates the rooftop before smothering the sky in smog. The night becomes starless, an empty expanse. The folk of the village cling tight.

The Straw Man tears tufts from the bales and tosses them into the fire. But with each the smoke comes thicker, burning his lungs and blackening the sky. As the smoke settles above all, the woods become shrouded, the village unseen. The Straw Man collapses to the floor.

He brings his hands together, praying to fade fast in the fumes, but feels discomfort in the tips of his fingers. Straining against the smoke, he inspects each and sees intrusion. Beneath his flesh: splinters. He rubs them gently and they squirm.

At the top of each finger, just beneath the nail, a spindle of gold extends from a pinprick. He pushes against one and it pushes back: a sliver of the auriferous inside himself.

Taking a strand between forefinger and thumb, the Straw Man starts to extract. He feels it worm passage along his finger, and as the splinter stings, he draws further and further, until with one final strain—straw. The smoke seems to subside.

He looks it over, so delicate, so clear in worth beneath its red mask. By instinct, he feeds it gently to the furnace, and as the end singes, he glimpses scarlet, before the straw is taken up in a blaze.

The Straw Man tears the strands from each finger. He folds them over into themselves but cannot tie the noose. Beneath the flesh of his arm he sees more material, starting just below the wrist, ending just before the elbow.

He pinches the skin and pushes against the straw; sees it pierce through with ease. Tearing it out, it twists beneath his arms, tangling with tendons as he withdraws another golden lock. In his thigh he sees more, his neck, his chest; yet more in his shoulder, waist, ankle, cheek; stomach, liver, bones, blood.

As he takes from his legs, he relies on the bales for support; as he takes from his lungs, he gasps each breath; as he takes from his brain, hard to think. Withdraw, fold; withdraw, wrap; withdraw, cut; withdraw, bind; withdraw, cinch; withdraw, pierce; complete.

In his bloodied hands, half torn away, the Straw Man cradles his final effigy. The scarlet smoke will come. It must.

Simulacrum

1.

'The image of literature to be found in contemporary culture is tyrannically centred on the author, his person, his history, his tastes, his passions.'

—ROLAND BARTHES, 'The Death of the Author'

Wallace first read *Simulacrum* a few decades ago, as an undergraduate at Oxford. It was shortly after his first encounters with Freud, Lacan, Barthes and Foucault; just as he was beginning to learn of the approach to literature not as a *who*, but as a *what.* The both timeless and timely tale of young Camille navigating the sphere of Parisian high society within which she no longer found herself its centre; meeting a man, Timothée, who occupied so much lower a station, but who appeared so much more secure; and then the sadness of their sudden misfortunes. It appeared old-fashioned—it was, even for its time—but still it seemed to resonate.

Yet it was not *Simulacrum*'s narrative which sustained critical interest, with journal articles, keynote lectures, blog posts, think pieces and theses all dedicated to decoding it. It was not the plot which held even Wallace's own. It was the anonymity of the Author. Still, just over two hundred years after its initial publication, the text held no attribution, nobody to whom to subscribe the genius of the work. Whoever he was, and Wallace was certain it was a he, he went undiscovered during his lifetime and those which followed.

Wallace often considered the kind of man he must have been. Strong in stature and stern in spirit, as with all Authors of his day. Perhaps he was born into high society himself, thus accounting for his voracious knowledge of that milieu. Raised with a distant father and a doting mother, or, though less probably, the inverse; but certainly, one parent close and the other closed off, with the latter replaced by a nanny, a carer, or the like.

What was clearest, however, were the preferences he held as a writer; a love for the quirks of language. The often misquoted, 'My dear, would you care to take a walk?', 'A walk? I have walked this path a dozen times and waver each and always', presented an Author who relished in duplexity. And then there was the subject matter itself: scandalous in its own time, and still challenging common decency today. Alongside the later Zola and Mirbeau, he had certainly helped to shock the literary bourgeoisie out of their collective conservatism.

It was these themes which had led to Wallace's devotion to decrypting *Simulacrum.* To name but the most recent of his works, he had published *The Feminine Fallacy: Sex and Simulacrum*; *First and Last: Why Simulacrum's First Edition Must be Found*; and his edited collection, *The Cambridge Companion to Simulacrum.* In each of these works, he considered the text in all of its guises, constructing an Author at once ethereal and evidenced.

In the absence of the Author, Wallace was widely regarded as the authoritative voice on *Simulacrum.*

2.

'To give an Author to a text is to impose a stop clause, to furnish it with a final signification, to close the writing.'

—ROLAND BARTHES, 'The Death of the Author'

Following a symposium in Senate House on the literary preoccupations of the years 1810 through to 1820, Wallace wandered the streets of London alone. He had heard papers including, 'The Pride Before the Fall: Darcy's Sins in Jane Austen's *Pride and Prejudice* (1813)', and 'Freak Show: Mary Shelley's *Frankenstein* (1818) and Myths of Disfigurement'. His own, discussing what the characters of *Simulacrum* revealed of their creator, had been a success, though it largely treaded familiar ground. There was, after all, little more to say.

As he walked, he passed by a bookstore specialising in the supernatural and the occult: tarot readings, folklore, Wicca and other such mysticisms. Giving it no more than a brief indulgence, with this being of no particular interest to him, Wallace made to continue. But then a rather short and ragged gentleman, thirty at the most, stopped him.

'Excuse me,' he said, offering his hand while the other held to a walking stick. There was some dirt beneath his fingernails. The kind of man unfortunate enough to be begging or petitioning a questionnaire, Wallace assumed. The kind who would not know the nineteenth century from the eighteenth, let alone which he lived in now. 'I'm sorry, but I must speak with you.'

'You weren't at the conference, were you?' Wallace replied, and, needing no answer, walked away.

The next day, Wallace fancied a short break from study, with his latest work not quite progressing as quickly as he had hoped. Though he was confident in the concept, he was finding it increasingly difficult to argue that critics should simply stop arguing about *Simulacrum*. It was exhausted, resolved. His work complete. So, having turned to nature to restore in himself that which simply typing failed to uncover, Wallace walked through Walpole Park.

As he passed the lake and made for the other, where the fountain's streams stilled and self-doubt he found surfacing; as he ambled across the green where dog-walkers tossed frisbees, couples created shared photography, and new mothers and fathers aired their children; he saw in the distance, at the far end of the grass, that very same man.

Though the haze of the sun blurred his outline, Wallace could just discern his figure, warping into the waters behind. With one hand firmly upon that same cane, the other waved greeting, beckoning him closer.

The thought occurred to Wallace that he should make as he had done previously and divert his course, returning to his day by a more circuitous and more comfortable route. But there was something about this man which intrigued him. From afar, Wallace thought he appeared almost in image like Berche, the Shylockian or Faganesque figure from *Simulacrum* to whom Dickens was undoubtedly indebted. Indeed, this very moment reminded Wallace more and more of the garden scene towards the text's climax, when Berche is slain by Timothée. Still reticent, he approached.

'Hello,' he said cautiously.

'Hello,' the man returned. 'Nice day, isn't it?'

He spoke in an accumulated London accent not dissimilar from Wallace's own. The kind which sounded as if it never truly belonged to the speaker but was simply on loan. Wallace failed to be convinced that under the circumstances these pleasantries were particularly pleasant, but evidently having had the same thought, the man laughed slightly. 'Excuse me. But, as I said before, I really must speak with you.'

'About what?' Wallace asked. 'Why me?'

The man spoke his name and said, '*Simulacrum.*' The word sounded almost unfamiliar to Wallace. 'Is there anywhere we could talk in private? I really must speak with you.' His inflection and intonation never changed.

Though Wallace was far from convinced that this would be a discussion which merited privacy—though far from a bestseller, *Simulacrum* was still a modest success in its time, remaining a curio in critical circles and regularly appearing in and out of print—Wallace did know of a pub nearby which could provide such peace, while also being suitably public to ensure his safety.

More than anything, he was pleased to be recognised, to discuss his work further. Academics grew increasingly dull, especially as symposia dragged on. A fresh argument, a fresh approach, from a non-academic with a new angle, seemed just the thing that might save Wallace's work. Perhaps he had judged this man too soon.

The Workshop was but a few minutes' walk away. Wallace led onwards, and with the clunk of his cane regularly hitting the pavement beside him, the man followed.

3.

'The birth of the reader must be ransomed by the death of the Author.'

—ROLAND BARTHES, 'The Death of the Author'

Wallace had visited the Workshop more than his fair share during his time in London. He had become faintly familiar with the patrons and the owners, a couple called the Wrights who held weekly quizzes, monthly jazz sessions and other such crowd-drawing events. As such, he was able to swiftly usher themselves into the private function room to continue their conversation in solitude. It was far too big for their needs, but it was practical, nevertheless. Wallace suggested drinks, which to his surprise the man bought—not a beggar after all—and then they settled down in earnest.

'Attlick,' he introduced, raising his glass. Wallace raised his in return, eager to hear a new perspective. 'Thank you. I know this is all very strange. If not my knowing you, then certainly my knowing of where to find you. But I am certain what I have to say will be of great interest.' He shuffled on his chair, either out of eagerness or discomfort.

Though admittedly strange, Wallace did not think it was too out of the ordinary that he might be recognised for his work. But conmen do exist, he had read as much, and so he eyed Attlick carefully. He hoped to detect a tick or a tell that might fault his façade, but Attlick maintained his eye, moment for moment, and slowly Wallace warmed to the man.

'You see, I have read a great deal on *Simulacrum*. Everything from sexuality to racialism to theological allegory to psychogeography. Marxist, feminist, post-colonialist, new historicist. But whatever I read, the thoughts only lingered so long before they reverted to the same tired husk: not what, never what, but *who*.'

'It is one of the last critical debates remaining,' Wallace said. 'Like

Jack the Ripper.'

'Yes, and I fail to see why. When I read *Simulacrum*, which I do less and less as the days go by, I find myself in constant conflict. Camille, to me, seems a stranger, one I am never convinced I will fully know. Timothée I grasp slightly clearer, but even he does things which surprise and disturb me in every reading. If you'll forgive the sentiment, *Simulacrum* seems almost unstable.'

The thought crossed Wallace's mind that maybe Attlick had not read his works, after all, for he had easily explained such things early on in his career. Maybe he was beyond the reach of amateur scholars. But instead he said, 'The characters are elusive. It had been written about a great deal whether the narrators can be trusted, and their arcs are as told.'

'Yes,' Attlick replied. 'Except it hasn't. It has been written that Camille appears a stranger, but only so as to consider what kind of a man would portray the female so. It has been written that Timothée acts out of disparate interests, but solely to unmask the deviser of his desires. Even Berche has been branded indicative of a man abused. The characters are always just augurs, the plot a scattering of runes, divining that great, elusive *who*.'

'Well, if he is not in the characters or the plot, we can see little of him elsewhere,' Wallace said, purely to challenge the man. To his surprise, however, Attlick agreed.

'We can see him *nowhere*. I know you hold the work in great esteem, I have read as much in your own words. But I fear that it is not the work you admire, but the worker.' Wallace raised his brow. 'That is why I am here, so that you can dispel all of this. To put an end to it.' He said Wallace's name again. 'I wrote *Simulacrum*.'

Wallace failed to restrain his laughter at this, the beer bubbling slightly between his lips. Attlick looked at him as if he might have expected such a response and smiled warmly.

'I did not realise I was talking to a corpse,' Wallace said. 'You look well. How old must you be?'

'Two hundred and three,' he said. 'Supposedly.'

Despite this improving Wallace's mood considerably, he now failed to see any further point to the conversation. Though not quite in the way he had expected, it had clarified the trajectory of his latest thesis, and so he was eager to return to work. Thanking him for the drink, at least, Wallace rose from his chair and made to leave. But then Attlick, leaning forward in his own, said, 'Please, indulge me for a second. Say that it was true. What would you ask of me?'

The hypothetical was interesting enough that Wallace stopped to give it some thought, wavering in the doorway. It took a few minutes before he answered, 'I suppose...I suppose I would ask, "Why romance?".' I have reconciled almost everything else in the text with meaning: the intertextuality of the clergy's names and the Concordat; the symbolism of the chosen architecture; the prophet who portends the Hundred Days; even the sporadic intrusion of the unidentifiable, unrelated voice. But the central premise...it had been done. Why choose to repeat it?'

'For exactly that,' Attlick replied. 'Because it had been done before.'

Wallace was fully set on leaving now, going to talk with one of the Wrights instead, perhaps. But Attlick seemingly paid no heed to this and continued.

'Because it had been done before, but not perfectly, and that made it easier. I had yet to see it written in exactly the way which I was doing, had yet to see the elements combined into what became *Simulacrum*. *René*, the Bible, as is still required now, even de Sade. It's all in there. The book hardly belongs to me.'

Wallace stared at him, incredulous. He was evidently a scholar of some regard, but increasingly hard to place. Wallace watched as he withdrew a pen and a handkerchief from one of his pockets and etched his signature upon it. He slid the handkerchief across the table. Wallace returned to his seat.

The name was pristine and written in cursive, a handwriting no longer in fashion or function.

'Really now, this proves nothing,' Wallace said, and then from within his coat Attlick produced a book. The first edition of *Simulacrum.*

It was well documented that such a text existed; Wallace himself had written on it. The supposed only manuscript which identified the Author. But he had had every copy burned before they went to market so as to preserve his identity, perhaps out of uncertainty of his own skill. Fraud briefly flicked through Wallace's mind, but that which Attlick produced was real: it moulted to Wallace's touch, and on the first page was that same signature.

Questions rushed to Wallace:

'Camille's father, was he—'

'Guilloton and Louis?' Attlick replied. 'An amalgamation of them both, if you prefer.'

'And her mother?'

'A monarchist, if you please…though never voiced.'

'The time period?'

'Deliberately unspecified, though I know you've found the rhetoric of revolution hardly subtle.'

'And Camille?'

'Take ever romantic heroine, make them the hero, and then see where you think it leads.'

Over the next twenty minutes the questions continued thus. Wallace found all his suppositions confirmed, those he had proposed and those he had held to himself. Suddenly, he bore the cipher and the work seemed to illuminate: the truth had simply been there. But he found he had overlooked the obvious.

'But how can you? How can you be here?'

'The book is still read.'

'But does that mean? Shelley? Austen? Balzac? Hoffmann? Are they all still alive?'

'No, no, they put their names to their works. Though Austen nearly got away with it.'

'Then what about Eliot? Or the Brontës?'

'Eventually uncovered,' Attlick said. Wallace felt a tinge of remorse in his voice.

'So you're? The Author?' he asked.

Attlick never confirmed or denied it. For a moment he seemed to stop. Wallace watched him carefully. His face had stilled. His eyes no longer matched Wallace's own but simply stared out into a singular space. His mouth was slightly limp and his breaths—well, he appeared not to be breathing at all. And then he was back. His gaze returned to Wallace's.

'Who *are* you?' Wallace asked.

'I am the writer.' Attlick's speech had altered from before. It was no longer erudite, but, stilted, somehow. Pained.

'Where were you born?' Wallace asked. 'How were you raised?'

'I am the writer.' The words were broken and harsh, rasps coming from a dried and tired throat.

'What led you to write *Simulacrum*? To write?'

'I am the man who writes.'

Text and Author were closing off from Wallace with each passing second, with so much unresolved. He attempted to refresh Attlick's memory with more and more questions, simple ones, but the answers only repeated. Yet, the more questions Wallace asked, the more he knew.

'Why demonise Berche?'

'I am the writer.'

'Because to demonise the ruling class would risk playing the hand of revolution too clearly; would risk alienating the readership, also. What did you mean when the unidentifiable voice laments, "even the

Fates could not prevent their own"?'

'I am the man who writes.'

'To show that every character, even Camille, is ultimately a pawn to the whims of a society leaving them behind. Surely?'

'The writer…the man who writes.'

Wallace asked and asked, tearing *Simulacrum* apart and then reconstructing it. And with each and every response Attlick gave, each pained admission, *Simulacrum* seemed to solve itself.

But as those answers came, Attlick's rasps became hoarser, fainter, until Wallace leant ever closer to hear. On each brief occasion Wallace considered the man before him, he seemed to have aged a decade; hair thinning, eyes growing glassy, hands regressing to bone and his grasp upon his cane becoming not accessory but appendage. His spine curved, and he seemed to shrink, diminishing with each of Wallace's questions until, and he knew not when, his questions were asked, and his answers returned, but the call of the writer came not.

Wallace was alone, with the text upon the table. Attlick's glass was empty, the sunhat and cane gone with him. Wallace cast his mind to all he had written, the Author he had constructed. *Simulacrum* seemed a work he would never know.

A Burial At Sea

When she awoke, the words weighed heavy upon her. Spines cut into her ribs. Covers dug into her arms. Pages pressed down on her shoulders. Her legs were long since dead. Only her head and neck were granted movement, but with that came a penance of pain; a stinging from her forehead, as if by some blunt trauma. She must have been bleeding, once.

Surrounding her was a pandemonium of colour; of blacks and greys and greens and blues. Ambers, coppers and golds seared through the confusion, yet the white light above her subsumed all into itself. She thought that she was awaiting autopsy, soon to be dissected and discarded; soon to be judged by an unseeable overseer. The light blinded her whenever she glanced too close.

When her sight finally returned, she saw the sea of books which immured her; a cragged surface like a shore or frozen waves. The sea drift carried a scent of impossible age—of mouldering mingled with dust; mulched paper and marzipan. They extended for what must have been miles, creating a horizon entirely their own. No dying sun, no waning moon. Only the topography of text.

Shakespeare. Dante. Homer. Salinger. Bradbury. Ballard. Vonnegut. Chaucer.

Above, the ceiling was close; so close it seemed to weigh further upon her. The blinding white light was a glass skylight. Below, she could not fathom, immediate or endless; the books building up one atop the other. But she was within no secure surface, of that she was sure. One slip could cause collapse.

Though she could see nothing beyond except the books below and the ceiling above, extending endlessly like an overcast sky, she forced herself to believe that somewhere beyond her sightline stood cylindrical walls. She was enclosed within some silo, some structure, soundproof and silent. It would have been pointless to scream.

But, by fate or by mercy, she had been buried in its centre.

Whitehead. Conrad. Nabokov. Ibsen. Brecht. Faulkner. Dostoevsky. Joyce.

She tried to move her arms, immutable under the weight of the ocean. She tried to wriggle free, to position herself differently, but she was frozen in place: a marionette whose master had grown weary of play. All she could do was observe the books surrounding her, in slight peaks and smaller valleys. Those within which she found herself inmate.

Most had their covers facing the ceiling, revealing the pioneers who produced her prison:

Dos Passos. Fitzgerald. Walpole. Wyndham. Machen. Blackwood. Forster. Wells.

Anderson. Ishiguro. Byron. Murakami. Plato. Burgess. Borges. Chekhov.

Wilde. Poe. Stevenson. Dickens. Kerouac. Capote. Melville. McCarthy.

The list was exhaustive but far from exhausted.

Their designs portrayed a vastness of imagined worlds and individual experiences. The Earth divided into two and a man on fire; a panoptic eye, a self-portrait, a cockroach, New York; a labyrinth, a fly, a family hanging from a hand; an archway, a girl, the words *Ulysses, Lolita.*

Meanwhile, those texts that had split open onto random pages weaved together into a new work: *and as in one who falls, without knowing how, then a noise from the hall like a clash of china made them all listen, so the tale of confessions and executions went on, until there was a pile of corpses lying, the same flesh and blood as one's self! And none other will know of them until he dies.*

Authors and texts had coalesced into confinement; a junkyard of words manifesting as a jail. She looked out beyond the sea, her eyes tracing the ceiling. She hoped to pinpoint where it ceased or severed.

Instead, far in the distance, she thought she saw another white light, an echo of the one hanging over her. Her eyes darted between the one above and afar; the light seemed to stream in the same direction. Looking out, looking below, she tried to see a form like her own. There was only text after text after text.

Still, the thought stuck; the skylights repeated across the span of the silo. She was but one of many buried in this swamp, looking up at the slightest light, at freedom. There were no walls, no end in sight. She could no longer imagine where she fell.

If there were others, they would not have escaped. Some would have drowned; submerged, suffocated, and succumbed to whatever lurked below. Their attempts at liberation would have caused ripples in the sea which resolved near another in a roar. One's ascent would condemn another, and all would eventually sink. She lay in a mass grave.

Perhaps, just inches below her, were the bones of a hand which had tried desperately to find purchase in a sea that swallowed her whole. Or perhaps those living texts kept those below alive, an existence of no light spent reading and rereading the bars of their imprisonment. Or they had been consumed by the works, become part of this heaving wilderness. Fuel, for the old texts to live on. Not a grave, but a garden.

She thought of those ripples not as escapes, but as breaths; that she had been sacrificed to the maw of a beast. This was a feeding ground for something much greater.

Behind her, she thought she could see the sea parting. She tried to turn but could look only out of the corners of her eyes. The books seemed to bulge forth in a stream, sending others sideways. The sea split like a shark does the waters.

Whatever lurked beneath never came. She was thankful she had not screamed. But time, it seemed, was short.

Using her forehead, her chin, her teeth, she cleared the books in front of her. She nudged those which collared her neck, tumbling them a few inches away and sending shudders through the sea. Those which were more difficult to dislodge she bit into, tasting pulp. She clamped onto their covers and sent them skipping away like stones.

She continued nudging those she could and biting those she could not, when the sound of her struggle was buried beneath burrowing. Once more without her eyeline. Once more coming close before silence.

She sped up as best she could, until the crests of the waves surrounding her had grown in height, now an inch or so away. Her shoulders were freed at last, the pressure partly relieved, but any attempt to continue was Sisyphean. The books were now beyond her reach.

She flexed her hands within the waters, tensing to restore life. There was slight space to manoeuvre between the smooth of the pages and the rough of the bindings, and, pushing as hard as she could against the pressure, she burst her arms free.

As she did so, the waves broke. The books barrelled down and tightened around her waist and ribs. Far off, she thought she heard a scream.

Though her legs were still lost, and the breaths came shorter, she started to claw her way out of the mire. She dug her arms in deep and prepared to pull, pressed her nails into the offspring of the fathers. It would bring the texts close, raise the pressure upon herself so much that something might break; when she breathed out, they would press in. But then that burrowing came behind her and the sea screamed in approach. She pulled and pulled until something came loose and she dragged her legs free to the surface.

When she looked back, a pit the size of herself was sealing; churning jaws with texts as jagged teeth. When feeling finally returned to her, she brought herself up, standing upon the sea.

Mann. Synge. Twain. Huxley. Orwell. Tolstoy. Wordsworth. Kafka.

She looked down and tried to imagine what was beneath her. A wasteland of history, of thoughts and concepts, within which something still lived. She looked around at the other lights, another now visible to her left, and considered walking towards them. One's ascent condemned another only if they did not help.

But when she looked again to the skylight, it had withdrawn far beyond her; a mile out of reach; a flicker of light. The silo had stretched itself further, had grown with her inside. And then the groan of a sluice: from above, the books fell.

Catharsis

We met in the Workshop. Four of us, before word got out. We sat in a circle and slivers of paper were passed around — receipts, letters, torn-up posters. We wrote what we could never say. We scrunched up those papers and threw them to the floor, took one each at random.

Then the breaths. Sharply in, slowly out; sighs which relieved, resigned, accepted; the occasional laugh. We would stare at those papers for as long as we could: torn edges, a crease, a stain. When we saw each other, tears would be braced or granted reprieve; eyes would dart to anything but eyes; some would never open. Then the shuffle of bags, coats, chairs.

The Writers' Block

Floor 23. Workshop 8.

Michael sat in his studio, sustained only by the glare of artificial blue light. Beneath him, beside him, typewriters, keyboards and printers churned in a frenzy, the Workshops synced in sound over years of creation. Above, those sounds came slower. A solemn stillness from the middle floors.

Three desks comprised his study, each nailed to the floor and arranged in a triangle so that his works were written in isolation. He followed his muse to whichever desk, whichever work, he knew was ready to progress, and there he wrote until the words exhausted. On the leftmost desk there was a computer, where his fingers typed faster than his thoughts could follow. On the right, a tablet, out of ease. And at the desk at which he now sat, at the base of this arrangement, pen and paper were placed perpendicular.

Through iteration to iteration, writing and rewriting, drafting and redrafting, the residents of the Block produced. A successful work might catch on with the Market, ascending them a couple floors; a misfire would send them back to the start. And for those to whom the words, the writing, had ceased to come; time ticked short on their standings.

Michael was one of these Writers. Like everyone else who signed up—different backgrounds, same desires—he hoped to make it to the top. He had welcomed an environment of retreat without recreation; of residence without resort. In the Block, those who wrote became Writers. But the Block was no home to those who did not write.

During his time, Michael had written four pieces, progressing slowly up the storeys. He had not gotten far, with each work being only a minor success in the eyes of the Market, but still he had ascended.

Now, he divided his time between three more tales. A woman coming to terms with a sentient sea; a satire of the nuclear family set during the Cold War; and a masked autobiography of his own experiences in the Block.

But for each his instruments stalled; pages half complete. Without them, ascent was out of reach, and entropy, that gradual decay of name and note which cast so many from the Block, was inevitable.

Looking out of the single window of the Workshop, Michael saw the Thames settling to sleep. He scratched the skin of his arm, rapped his fingers against his desk, staring at the six words on his page. *To Matthew, words no longer came.*

Burnt out and exhausted, Michael had come to regard each of his works as word counts. The sea—1893—was far away in the future. The nuclear family—22,581—but a fourth finished. The autobiography: those six words.

Michael flitted from desk to desk, from story to story, hoping that time devoted to one might free up his thoughts for another. But nothing came.

And neither will it for me.

Try again. Fail again. Fail better.

The Writers' Block
Second Draft

Floor 23. Workshop 8.

You sit in your studio, enclosed within chipped concrete walls. Grey and giving way to the wind outside, the room is sustained only by blue light. Beneath you, beside you, typewriters, keyboards and printers churn in a frenzy; pencils scratch and pens click. Above, those sounds come slower. The peaceful purgatory of the middle floors.

Three desks comprise your study, each nailed to the floor and arranged in a triangle so that side-projects can be streamlined away. You follow your muse to whichever desk, whichever work, you know that you can break through, before shifting to a different station. On the leftmost desk there is a computer. On the right, a tablet. And at the desk at which you now sit, pen and paper face one another.

Through iteration to iteration, writing and rewriting, drafting and redrafting, the residents of the Block produce. A successful work might catch on with the Market, ascending them a couple floors; a misfire snakes them back to the start. And for those to whom the words, the writing, cease to come; legacy only lasts so long.

You are one of these Writers. Like everyone else who signs up—the would-be and the once were—you hope to make it to the top. Moving south to the city, you welcomed an environment of retreat without recreation; of residence without resort. In the Block, those who write become Writers. But it is no home to those who do not.

During your time, you have written four pieces. Creeping, more than climbing, up the Block. With each work only a minor success in the eyes of the Market, you have progressed little, but still you have ascended.

Now, you divide your time between three more tales. A real time consideration of one man awaiting the gallows; an immortal future society where only through drugs could one find death; and a veiled autobiography of your own experiences in the Block.

But each of these works escapes you. Without them, ascent is out of reach: entropy inevitable.

You look out of the Workshop to see the Thames settling to sleep. London, ever alive and thriving, so ignorant to the wants of the water. You rap your fingers against the desk, your forehead, your desk, back against your forehead, staring at the six words renting your page: *To Matthew, words no longer came.*

The last of your creativity spent, you regard each of your works as word counts. The gallows—893—is far from complete. Immortality—2581—out of reach. The autobiography: those six words.

You flit from desk to desk, from story to story, hoping that time devoted to one might free up your thoughts for another. But nothing comes. Each story has stagnated, your implements consumed by rust.

Before you signed up, you had heard the stories of the Block. You had heard of the successes, reaching the top with universally regarded novels and prize-winning collections; the hardest working, the most dedicated, the most driven Writers. Those whose names yours would be written alongside.

But you had also heard the stories of the rest. Those dedicated Writers, driven down to the bottom of the Block and beyond by entropy. Some struggled in return to their previous lives, others tried in vain to return. All never wrote again. Whatever form the symptoms took, entropy was always the cause.

You see your reflection in the window, drowned and dissolved in the Thames. Back home, you had heard the story of a woman who salvaged the suicidal from those waters, always too late or too soon. It was a selfless job by a selfless person. The Block above stood selfish.

You turn back to write, but still no words come.

A blank space. An impotent page. The nothing of anything.

Try again. Fail again. Fail—

The sound of creation comes.

Not the sound of pen upon paper. Not the light clicks of computer keys, nor the vibrations of a tablet. The sound of great, grinding impacts; of a whirring and ringing which pierces through the Block.

You see the other two desks beside you: barren, bereft, instruments stilled and still stalling. Yet the noise continues to come. A constant sound of grinding cogs and machinery, looping, replicating, forever repeating. It is directly behind you, always at the back of your mind. An indeterminable distance away. An incalculable closeness behind.

Turning around, you see a desk. Not the one to your left nor the one to your right, but existing between them both. A fourth, directly before you, flitting in and out of reality. One moment it is transparent, the next concrete, existing within impossible space. Forcing its way into the Workshop.

Atop, in an identical position to the instruments of your own, sits a typewriter. The keys are pressing themselves, churning out content, the paper replenishing itself as the words spill out. Stories of a self-obsessed self; of the gallows, the sea, immortality and war; of you and the Block. Each is there while the sound keeps coming. The sound of your own inability.

In the midst of this phasing, a form appears, hunched over the desk. A body, your body, pressing the keys at a feverish pace. Their fingers bleed. Their smile is wide.

You cannot hide, Michael. What will happen has already happened.

The Writers' Block
Third Draft

Floor 23. Workshop 8.

Michael sat in his studio, enclosed within chipped concrete walls. Grey and giving way to the wind outside, the room was sustained only by blue light. Beneath him, beside him, typewriters, keyboards and printers churned in a frenzy; pencils scratched and pens clicked. Above, those sounds came slower. The peaceful purgatory of the middle floors.

Four desks comprised his study, each nailed to the floor and arranged in a **diamond** so that side-projects could be streamlined away. He followed his muse to whichever desk, whichever work, he **thought** that he could break through, before **failing,** shifting to a different station. On the leftmost desk there was **nothing**. On the right, **nothing**. And at the desk at which he now sat, **nothing**. **Atop the fourth desk, a typewriter.**

Through iteration to iteration, writing and rewriting, drafting and redrafting, the residents of the Block produced. A successful work might catch on with the Market, ascending them a couple floors; a misfire would snake them back to the start. And for those to whom the words, the writing, had ceased to come; legacy only lasted so long.

Michael **would never be** one of these Writers. Like everyone else who signed up—the would-be and the once were—he **thought he could** make it to the top. Moving south to the city, he had welcomed an environment of retreat without recreation; of residence without resort. In the Block, those who wrote became Writers. It was no home to **Michael**.

During his time, Michael had written **nothing**. **Coasting,** more than climbing, up the Block. With each work a **failure** in the eyes of the Market, he had progressed nowhere, and so he had descended.

Now, he divided his time between three more failures. A real time consideration of one man unable to write; an immortal future society where nobody could write; and a veiled autobiography of his own failures.

But each of these works escaped him. Without them, ascent was out of reach: entropy inevitable.

Michael looked out of the wide-open window to see the Thames settling to sleep, almost welcoming. London, ever alive and thriving, so ignorant to the wants of the water. He rapped his fingers against his desk, his forehead, his desk, his forehead, his desk, his forehead, harder and harder, staring at the six words renting his page. To Michael, words would never come.

The last of his creativity spent, Michael had come to regard each of his works as failures. The gallows—zero—would never be complete. Immortality—zero—forever out of reach. The autobiography: but six words.

He flitted from desk to desk, from story to story, hoping that time devoted to one might free up his thoughts for another. But nothing came. Each story had stagnated, his implements consumed by rust. Michael had failed.

Before he signed up, Michael had heard the stories of the Block. He had heard of the successes, reaching the top with universally regarded novels and prize-winning collections; the hardest working, the most dedicated, the most driven Writers. Those whose names Michael's would never be written alongside.

But he had also heard the story of himself. That undedicated Writer, driven down to the bottom of the Block and beyond by inability. He struggled in his return to his previous life. He tried in vain to return. He never wrote again. Whatever form the symptoms took, his inability was the cause.

Michael saw his reflection in the window, drowned and dissolved in the Thames. Back home, he had heard the story of a woman who salvaged the suicidal from those waters, always too late or too soon. It was a selfish job by a selfish person. The Block above stood strong.

Michael turned back to write, but still no words would come. A blank space. An impotent page. The nothing of anything.

Fail again. Fail again. Fail again.

~~The sound of creation came.~~

~~Not the sound of pen upon paper. Not the light clicks of computer keys, nor the vibrations of a tablet. The sound of great, grinding impacts; of a whirring and ringing which pierced through the Block.~~

~~Michael could see the other two desks beside him: barren, bereft, instruments stilled and still stalling. Yet the noise continued to come. A constant sound of grinding cogs and machinery, looping, repeating, forever repeating. It was directly behind him, always at the back of his mind. An indeterminable distance away. An incalculable closeness behind.~~

~~Turning around, Michael saw a desk. Not the one to his left nor the one to his right, but existing between them both. A fourth, directly before him, flitting in and out of reality. One moment it was transparent, the next concrete, existing within impossible space. Forcing its way into the Workshop.~~

~~Atop, in an identical position to the instruments of Michael's own, sat a typewriter. The keys were pressing themselves, churning out content, the paper~~

~~replenishing itself as the words spilled out. Stories of a self obsessed self; of the gallows, the sea, immortality and war; of Michael and the Block. Each was there while the sound kept coming. The sound of his own inability.~~

~~In the midst of this phasing, a form appeared, hunched over the desk. A body, Michael's body, pressing the keys at a feverish pace. His fingers bled. His smile was wide.~~

I've tried deleting it, it's not work—

Michael turned back to his paper in the hope of retreat, of writing his way to safety. But the only words that existed, existed on the typewriter.

As that noise got louder, the shadow spoke.

'Failure...'

The Writers' Block
Eighth Draft

Floor 23. Workshop 8.

MichAel sat In his studio, encLosed within chipped concrete walls. Grey and giving way to the wind oUtside, the Room was sustainEd only by blue light. Beneath him, beside him, typewriters, keyboards and printers churned in a Frenzy; pencils scrAtched and pens clIcked. Above, those sounds came sLower. The peacefUl puRgatory of thE middle Floors.

Three desks comprised his study, eAch naILed to the floor and arranged in a triangle so that side-projects coUld be stREamlined away. He Followed his muse to whichever desk, whichever work, he knew thAt he could break through, before shIfting to a different station. On the Leftmost desk there was a compUteR. On thE right, a tablet. And at the desk at which he now sat, pen and paper FAced one another.

Through Iteration to iteration, writing and rewriting, drafting and redrafting, the residents of the BLock prodUced. A successful woRk might catch on with thE Market, ascending them a couple Floors; A mIsfire wouLd snake them back to the start. And for those to whom the words, the writing, had ceased to come; legacy only lasted so long.

Michael was one of these Writers. Like everyone else who signed Up—the would-be and the once weRE—he hoped to make it to the top. Moving south to the city, he had welcomed an environment oF retreAt wIthout recreation; of residence without resort. In the BLock, those who wrote became Writers. It was no home to those who did not.

DURing his timE, Michael had written Four pieces. Creeping, more thAn clImbing, up the BLock. With each work only a minor sUccess in the eyes of the MaRkEt, he had progressed little, but still he had ascended.

Now, he divided his time between three more tales. A real time consideration oF one mAn awaIting the gaLlows; an immortal futURE society where only through drugs could one Find deAth; and a veILed aUtobiogRaphy of his own Experiences in the Block.

But each oF these works escAped hIm. Without them, ascent was out of reach: entropy inevitabLe.

Michael looked oUt of the WoRkshop to sEe the Thames settling to sleep. London, ever alive and thriving, so ignorant to the wants of the water. He rapped his Fingers AgaInst his desk, his forehead, his desk, back against his forehead, staring at the six words renting his page. *To Matthew, words no* L*onger came.*

The last of his creativity spent, Michael had come to regard each of his works as word coUnts. The gallows—893—was faR from complEte. Immortality—2581—out oF reAch. The autobIography: those six words.

He fLitted from desk to desk, from story to story, hoping that time devoted to one might free Up his thoughts foR anothEr. But nothing came. Each story had stagnated, his implements consumed by rust.

BeFore he signed up, MichAel had heard the storIes of the BLock. He had heard of the sUccesses, REaching the top with universally regarded novels and prize-winning collections; the hardest working, the most dedicated, the most driven Writers. Those whose names yours would be written alongside.

But he had also heard the stories oF the rest. Those dedicAted WrIters, driven down to the bottom of the BLock and beyond by entropy. Some strUggled in theiR rEturn to their previous lives, others tried in vain to return. All never wrote again. Whatever Form the symptoms took, entropy wAs always the cause.

~~MIchaeL saw his reflection in the window, drowned and dissolved in the Thames. Back home, he had heard the story of a woman who salvaged the sUicidal fRom thosE waters, always too late or too soon. It was a selFless job by A selfless person. The Block above stood selfIsh.~~

~~MichaeL tURnEd back to write, but still no words would come. A blank space. An impotent page. The nothing of anything.~~

~~Try again. FAIL again. Fail—~~

I can't fix this.

The Writers' Block
Twenty-Third Draft

The sound of creation came.

Not the sound of pen upon paper. Not the light clicks of computer keys, nor the vibrations of a tablet. The sound of great, grinding impacts; of a whirring and ringing which pierced through the Block.

Michael could see the other two desks beside him: barren, bereft, instruments stilled and still stalling. Yet the noise continued to come. A constant sound of grinding cogs and machinery, looping, repeating, forever repeating. It was directly behind him, always at the back of his mind. An indeterminable distance away. An incalculable closeness behind.

Turning around, Michael saw a desk. Not the one to his left nor the one to his right, but existing between them both. A fourth, directly before him, flitting in and out of reality. One moment it was transparent, the next concrete, existing within impossible space. Forcing its way into the Workshop.

Atop, in an identical position to the instruments of Michael's own, sat a typewriter. The keys were pressing themselves, churning out content, the paper replenishing itself as the words spilled out. Stories of a self-obsessed self; of the gallows, the sea, immortality and war; of Michael and the Block. Each was there while the sound kept coming. The sound of his own inability.

In the midst of this phasing, a form appeared, hunched over the desk. A body, Michael's body, pressing the keys at a feverish pace. His fingers bled. His smile was wide.

Michael turned back to his paper in the hope of retreat, of writing his way to safety. But the only words that existed, existed on the typewriter.

As the noise got louder, the shadow spoke.

'Failure...' The word lasted for hours.

Defeated, Michael stood up from his chair and embraced the mirror of himself. He walked to the window, wide enough now for his own body, and placed his hands atop the ledge. He looked at all the floors he had ascended, and all those never to be reached. With one last look back, no reason to stay, he stood atop the ledge and leap—

No. This isn't the story.

The Writers' Block
Final Draft

Floor 23. Workshop 8.

Michael sat in his studio, enclosed within concrete walls. Sleep sacrificed to blue light, floaters finding root in his eyes, he had given his mind to the Block. Surrounding him were the sounds of machinery and automation; Writers churning content in cacophony. Above, those sounds came slower. Below, frenzied.

One desk comprised his study, from which all works were born. Atop it, pen and paper faced one another, with experiments discarded beneath. The wrong story, wrong voice; all were failures. But they were accepted. Learned from. Moved past.

Through iteration to iteration, drafting and redrafting, pruning and perfecting each and every paragraph, the residents of the Block produced. A successful work might catch on with the Market, ascending them a couple floors; a misfire would snake them back to the start. And for those to whom the words, the writing, had ceased to come; legacy only lasted so long.

Michael was one of these Writers. Like everyone else who signed up, he hoped to make it to the top. He had welcomed an environment of retreat without recreation; of residence without resort. In the Block, those who wrote became Writers. It was no home to those who did not.

During his time, he had written four pieces: tales of tortured artists and the torture of art. But his next work escaped him. A veiled autobiography of his own experiences in the Block, he had but six words: *To Matthew, words no longer came.*

And when the veil was lifted, that was the truth of it: A Writer who could no longer write.

Michael had heard the successes, reaching the top with universally regarded novels and prize-winning collections; the hardest working, the most dedicated, the most driven Writers. Those whose names his would be written alongside.

But those stories ignored how much the Block took. Concepts cannibalised into content. Writing commodified and carted out. So many burnt out Writers, buried and built into the Block. The Block made you a Writer, at the expense of wanting to write.

Yet as Michael looked out of the window of the Workshop, each light suggested a possibility, written outside of this world. There were more stories to share, more tales to tell; more modes, more genres, more forms. The sentient sea and the immortal future; the gallows and the nuclear family. Any life beyond this one was no longer an option. But there was life beyond the Block.